CRITICAL THINKING
— IN —
AMERICAN HISTORY™

Drafting the Constitution

Weighing Evidence to Draw Sound Conclusions

Kristin Eck

The Rosen Publishing Group, Inc., New York

Published in 2006 by The Rosen Publishing Group, Inc.
29 East 21st Street, New York, NY 10010

First Edition

Library of Congress Cataloging-in-Publication Data

Eck, Kristin.
Drafting the Constitution: weighing evidence to draw sound conclusions/
Kristin Eck.—1st ed.
    p. cm.—(Critical thinking in American history)
Includes index.
ISBN 1-4042-0412-1 (library binding)
1. United States. Constitution—Juvenile literature. 2. United States.
Constitution—Study and teaching (Secondary)—Juvenile literature.
3. United States—Politics and government—1775–1783—Juvenile literature.
4. United States—Politics and government—1775–1783—Study and
teaching (Secondary)—Juvenile literature. 5. United States—Politics and
government—1783–1789—Juvenile literature. 6. United States—Politics
and government—1783–1789—Study and teaching (Secondary)—
Juvenile literature. 7. Constitutional history—United States—Juvenile
literature. 8. Constitutional history—United States—Study and teaching
(Secondary)—Juvenile literature. I. Title. II. Series.
E303.E28 2006
342.7302'9—dc22

                                                        2005001192

Manufactured in the United States of America

On the cover: Left: Constitution Hall in Washington, D.C. Right: the
Liberty Bell, outside Independence Hall in Philadelphia, Pennsylvania.

Contents

A Tough Job

Do rough drafts, raised hands, differing opinions, hot heads, calm voices, brains, and bullies sound familiar? Does this remind you of your classroom? Imagine if you and a group of classmates had to write the rules for how the rest of the country would be run. Imagine if you had to do it in just four months! You have your own opinions. Your classmates have theirs. Different people have different perspectives, or ways of looking at things. Do you think you could sort out all the different opinions? Could you work together to write a document that American citizens would continue to live by for more than 200 years? That's just what the Founding Fathers did at the Constitutional Convention in Philadelphia in the hot summer of 1787.

Fact Finder

Make a list of ten questions about the United States Constitution. You might ask questions like these:

✓ How was it written?

✓ Why was it written?

✓ Who helped to write it?

Look for the answers as you read this book.

State delegates sign the U.S. Constitution in Philadelphia, Pennsylvania, on September 17, 1787.

The American Revolution

We have to back up a little to put the Constitutional Convention into perspective. Before there was a United States of America, there were thirteen separate colonies. Before there was a Constitution, there was the Articles of Confederation. And before there was a Constitutional Convention, there was an American Revolution!

From 1775 to 1783, American colonists fought the British to win their freedom and independence. The British had forced the colonies to pay taxes. The colonies thought it was unfair that they did not have a voice in the government that made rules for them. America would eventually win the war, but even before the fighting ended, the work of setting up a new country began. The newly established states needed to figure out how to work together. Politician John Dickinson and a committee were asked to draft a constitution to outline the powers of the individual states and those of the Continental Congress (the federal government). Dickinson

Think Tank

The last line of text on the opposite page contains a fact (red) and an opinion (blue).

✓ Form a group and list examples of how the colonies suffered under British rule.

✓ Discuss why you think the author's opinion is or is not valid.

✓ Explain and discuss what is meant by "the new American states did not want to repeat history."

✓ Draw up a list of suggestions about how the states could avoid repeating history.

American colonists and British soldiers engage in battle at Lexington, Massachusetts, on April 19, 1775. The battles at Lexington and Concord were the first of the Revolutionary War.

and his colleagues were well aware of the concerns about a central government having too much power. The colonies had suffered under the ironfisted rule of Great Britain, and the new American states did not want to repeat history.

The Articles of Confederation

The plan of government Dickinson and his colleagues developed was called the Articles of Confederation. It was submitted to the Second Continental Congress on July 12, 1776, on the heels of the Declaration of Independence. It was not approved by the states and made the law of the land until 1781. The Articles of Confederation created a "firm league of friendship" among the states. The balance of power definitely favored the individual states over the federal government, as these provisions of the articles show:

- Government measures had to be approved by nine of the thirteen states.
- The federal government could not tax states to raise money.
- The federal government did not have control over foreign trade.
- The federal government could make laws, but could not enforce them.
- Any change in the federal government's power had to be approved by all thirteen states.

Think Tank

✓ Pick a partner.

✓ One of you will role-play a member of the Continental Congress.

✓ One of you will role-play a member of the committee that wrote the articles.

✓ The member of Congress makes up five questions about the articles.

✓ The committee member answers those questions.

✓ Now switch roles.

The United States' first constitution was called the Articles of Confederation (right). It was adopted by the Continental Congress on November 15, 1777, to create "a firm league of friendship" among the thirteen individual states.

While the Articles of Confederation prevented the problem of a central government having too much power, it was still a flawed document. George Washington described the articles as "little more than the shadow without the substance."

The State of the Union

Like Americans today, Americans in the 1780s were not afraid to speak their minds. Americans were concerned about the state of the Union. Under the Articles of Confederation, each state operated more or less as a free agent. A "firm league of friendship" was a nice idea in theory. But it was hard to accomplish in practice, especially when dealing with issues like foreign and domestic trade (meaning commerce with other countries and within the United States).

In Congress, Charles Pinckney expressed his concern by suggesting that Congress consider revising the Articles of Confederation. Think about the American citizens of today. They write letters to their congressional representatives or even to the president. They sign petitions to let the government know how they feel about different issues. Pinckney was aware of citizens' concerns. He

Paper Works

Do you think a "firm league of friendship" would be an effective arrangement for the American states today? Why or why not?

Here are some things to think about as you write your response:

✓ What have you learned about America under the Articles of Confederation?

✓ Use your personal experience to inform your writing, too.

✓ Have you worked in a group? Was there a strong leader or was everyone an equal participant? How effectively did the group function?

voiced these concerns in Congress. A committee was formed to discuss the idea of revising the Articles of Confederation. One idea that came from the committee was to give Congress power over foreign and domestic trade. Another idea was to give Congress the power to tax the states. The ideas didn't get very far, though. Congress did not think the thirteen states would agree to any of the ideas, so they were not implemented.

Charles C. Pinckney of South Carolina *(above)* was educated in England but became a supporter of the patriot cause in 1775. A former royal militia officer, he served as a colonel in the First South Carolina Regiment during the revolution. As a congressman, he suggested that the Articles of Confederation be revised.

A solution was still needed. Trade continued to be a problem. The American economy was shaky, and the country needed to gain solid footing after the efforts and expenses of the American Revolutionary War.

The Annapolis Convention

A convention was called to take place in Annapolis, Maryland, in 1786. The agenda focused on America's trade problems. Nine of the thirteen states said they would participate in the Annapolis Convention, but only five states actually sent delegations. In response to the poor attendance, James Madison and Alexander Hamilton composed a letter to the American states, inviting them to attend another convention, which would have a broader agenda. This convention, which would take place in Philadelphia in May 1787, would cover not only trade issues, but also the federal government's overall role and powers.

The Continental Congress made the convention's agenda official by issuing the following resolution on February 21, 1787: ". . . it is expedient that on the Second Monday in May next a Convention of

Word Works

✓ **delegate** A person acting for another, such as a representative to a convention or conference.

✓ **delegation** A group of people chosen to represent others.

✓ **expedient** Suitable for achieving a particular end in a given circumstance; practical, or advisable.

"Delegate" is the root of "delegation." You could figure out what delegation means by knowing the meaning of the word "delegate." A delegation is a group of delegates.

The Annapolis Convention took place at the Maryland State House *(above)* in September 1786. The convention was held to discuss trade problems among the thirteen states.

delegates who shall have been appointed by the several states be held at Philadelphia for the sole and express purpose of revising the Articles of Confederation . . ."

A Date with History

Attendance at the Philadelphia Convention was much better than it had been at the Annapolis Convention. All of the states, with the exception of Rhode Island, sent delegations to what would become known as the Constitutional Convention. The men who made up these delegations would later be recognized, along with the writers of the Declaration of Independence, as the Founding Fathers of America. The group assembling at the Philadelphia State House on May 25, 1787, was about to make a critical contribution to the story of American history and democracy.

Seventy men had been invited to participate. Fifty-five men actually attended. Although the work of the Founding Fathers would lay the groundwork for freedom of speech, freedom of the press, and the public's right to know, the convention was cloaked in secrecy. The Philadelphia State House had guards stationed outside to ensure that the delegates could work in peace and privacy. The convention proceedings were to be kept a secret from the public until the work was done.

Q & A

✓ What were the practical reasons for keeping the proceedings of the convention secret from the public?

✓ Do you think the secrecy around the convention sent a good or bad message to the public? Explain your answer.

George Washington is best known as the commander-in-chief of the Continental army and the first president of the United States. Between these two important roles, he also served as president of the Constitutional Convention in 1787. He is seen here at his desk in Philadelphia's Independence Hall presiding over the convention proceedings.

The Men Behind the Pens

If you were selecting a group of friends and classmates to write the rules for how your school would be run, what kinds of criteria would you use to make sure the group reflected different viewpoints? It is interesting to think about this when you consider the qualities shared by the delegates to the Constitutional Convention. In terms of wealth, education, and political experience, the delegates shared a lot of common ground. For a group charged with designing the best, most effective national government possible, there was not too much diversity represented. In general, the delegates fit this profile:

- Well-educated and wealthy
- Lots of political experience
- Had held posts in local, county, colonial, or state governments

A few delegates could even boast these credentials:

- Signers of the Declaration of Independence or Articles of Confederation
- Members of the Continental Congress

Get Graphic

Check out this map of the original thirteen colonies and the portraits of some key delegates.

✓ Make a chart to organize information about the delegates shown.

✓ Are the delegates from Northern or Southern states?

✓ Are they from big or small states? (As the convention debates heat up, the size and location of states will affect the stand their delegates take on different issues!)

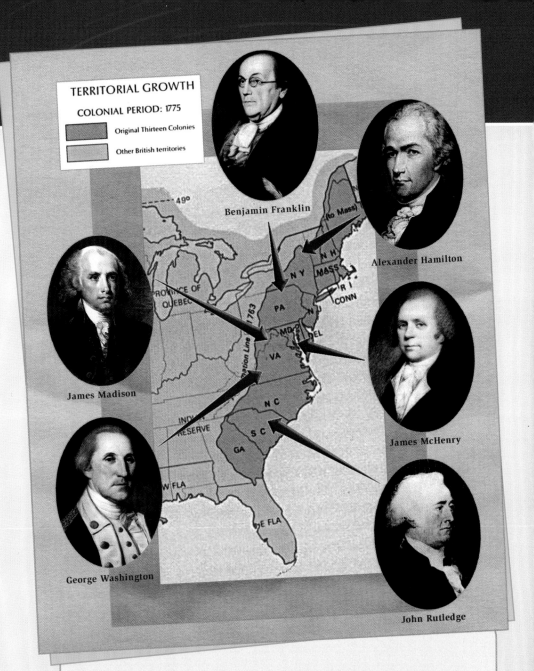

TERRITORIAL GROWTH

COLONIAL PERIOD: 1775

Original Thirteen Colonies

Other British territories

Benjamin Franklin

Alexander Hamilton

James Madison

James McHenry

George Washington

John Rutledge

The above map shows the boundaries of the thirteen states at the time of the Revolutionary War. Around the map are pictured several important delegates to the Constitutional Convention. Clockwise from top center are: Ben Franklin (Pennsylvania), Alexander Hamilton (New York), James McHenry (Maryland), John Rutledge (South Carolina), George Washington (Virginia), and James Madison (Virginia).

In the Spotlight

The assembled delegates were in the spotlight! There was a lot riding on the success of their efforts. Remember, the delegates reported to the Pennsylvania State House amid troubled times for a young America. War debts, trade problems, and even rebellion against the government, which seemed unable to support its struggling citizens, dominated the headlines. The Constitutional Convention hoped to offer solutions to these growing problems. One of the delegates, George Mason, wrote a letter to his son that reflected the pressure the delegates faced: "The Eyes of the United States are

Paper Works

Imagine you're a citizen in 1787 America writing a letter to a convention delegate.

✓ Outline your expectations for the convention.

✓ Practice different kinds of essay writing in the letter:

- Personal: Introduce yourself (What state are you from? What is your occupation? Did you play a role in the American Revolution?)

- Descriptive: Describe the current situation in your state (What's the economy like? What is the mood like? Are people satisfied with the government under the Articles of Confederation?)

- Issue-based: Explain the major issues you think the convention delegates should address; explain why you see them as priorities.

The clock and bell tower of Independence Hall can be seen rising above the bustling streets of late eighteenth-century Philadelphia, Pennsylvania. The Declaration of Independence, the Articles of Confederation, and the U.S. Constitution were all drafted and signed in this historic building, which still stands today.

turned upon this Assembly and their Expectations raised to a very anxious Degree. May God Grant that we be able to gratify them by establishing a wise and just government."

Getting Down to Business

George Washington, who had made a name for himself as a general in the American Revolution, was unanimously chosen to be the chairman of the convention. He had a reputation for being wise and coolheaded. Those qualities would come in handy when debates over controversial issues made the convention feel more like a battlefield. Major William Jackson of New Jersey was named secretary of the convention. He kept the official convention journal, recording attendance and votes.

The delegates met six days a week in sessions that lasted five to six hours each day. That's about the length of a school day. They had to do work outside the sessions, too. It was like they had homework! They read proposals, prepared speeches, and met in committees.

Many of the delegates kept their own journals during the convention, kind of like taking notes in class. They kept track of the many ideas and arguments so they could study them and decide how they would vote on different matters.

Word Works

✓ **controversial** Causing disagreement, dispute, or opposing views.

✓ **reputation** The way someone's character or personality is judged by other people.

✓ **unanimously** With the agreement and consent of all.

Journal of the federal Convention Monday July 16. 1787

The question being taken on the whole of the report from the grand Committee as amended

it passed in the affirmative

and is as follows, namely.

Resolved — That in the original formation of the Legislature of the United States the first Branch thereof shall consist of Sixty five members.

of which number

New Hampshire shall send	Three
Massachusetts	Eight
Rhode Island	One
Connecticut	Five
New York	Six
New Jersey	four
Pennsylvania	Eight
Delaware	One
Maryland	Six
Virginia	Ten
North Carolina	Five
South Carolina	Five
Georgia	Three

But as the present situation of the States may probably alter in the number of their inhabitants, the Legislature of the United States shall be authorized from time to time to apportion the number of representatives: and in case any of the States shall hereafter be divided, or enlarged by addition of territory, or any two or more States united, or any new States created within the limits of the United States the Legislature of the United States shall possess authority to regulate the number of repre- sentatives now in case any of the foregoing cases upon the principle of their number of inhabitants, according

The Virginia Plan

The summer of 1787 was an oppressively hot one in Philadelphia. Once the discussion got going in earnest, the temperature in the Philadelphia State House (not to mention the tempers) would only get hotter.

Edmund Randolph of Virginia sparked the first big debate, on Tuesday, May 29. He set off a political firecracker by presenting the so-called Virginia Plan. Before presenting the bold proposal, Randolph acknowledged the good intentions of the framers of the Articles of Confederation. But after that nod to the framers, he proceeded to list all the weaknesses of the articles and of America's current government. Randolph's comments made clear that he and his Virginia colleagues were proposing something far greater than a revision. They had a plan for a whole new government for the United States. Although Randolph introduced

Word Works

✓ **annihilate** To cause to be of no effect, or to destroy.

✓ **consolidate** To join together into a whole, or to unite.

✓ **sovereignty** Freedom from outside control, or being in a self-governing state.

Randolph used strong words to describe the intent of his plan. Can you try stating the plan's goal in your own words?

the Virginia Plan to the convention delegates, thirty-six-year-old James Madison of Virginia was the key author of the plan. Madison's ideas about a strong central government made up of three branches (legislative, executive, and judicial) anchored the plan. These branches would act as checks and balances, but this national government was designed to have greater power than state legislatures. Randolph explained that the plan "meant a strong consolidated union in which the idea of states should be nearly annihilated."

A manuscript page from the Virginia Plan, which proposed a new three-branch federal government with greater authority over individual states.

The Virginia Plan upset delegates concerned about preserving state sovereignty. The plan forced all the delegates to question whether they were ready to raise the stakes of the Constitutional Convention even higher. The delegates' assignment was to revise the Articles of Confederation. The Virginia Plan gave the delegates the task of creating a new government altogether. This was not what they had come to do. This was not what they had promised the people they represented. Would accepting this task be an act of patriotism or sabotage? For ten days, the delegates would wrestle with these issues.

The New Jersey Plan

The Virginia Plan highlighted the conflict of interest between big states and small states. Big states stood to gain from a strong national government in which they thought they could wield more power. A confederation of states, in which each state had equal power, better served small states' interests. William Paterson of New Jersey became a spokesperson for the small states with his intro-duction of the New Jersey Plan on June 13. This plan was more in keeping with the original mission of the Constitutional Convention. It suggested simply revising the Articles of Confederation. Specifically, the New Jersey Plan suggested the Continental Congress be allowed to do the following:

- Raise money through taxes
- Play a larger role in trade
- Make its laws and treaties binding on the states

Now there were two options on the table. Delegates could vote for the Virginia Plan, a radical

Think Tank

✓ Form two teams of classmates.

✓ One team supports the Virginia Plan.

✓ One team supports the New Jersey Plan.

✓ Have each side prepare and present arguments defending its plan.

✓ Ask class members in the audience to prepare questions for the teams and meet in small groups to decide how to vote.

✓ Will your classmates choose the Virginia Plan or the New Jersey Plan?

24

proposal to discard the Articles of Confederation and establish a strong central government. Or, delegates could cast their votes for the New Jersey Plan, which would keep things as they were but introduce measures to make the existing Continental Congress a more effective governing body. Opposing camps were beginning to form. The nationalists thought a strong central government could help America right itself from its downward spiral. The states' rights advocates wanted to keep the states out from under the thumb of an all-controlling central government.

William Paterson *(above)* offered an alternative to the Virginia plan. His proposal became known as the New Jersey Plan, named after the state he represented. It called for equal representation for each state in a single legislative body.

Put yourself in the delegates' shoes. They had to make tough decisions about the fate of a new nation, and they had to make the decisions quickly. The delegates argued over the New Jersey Plan for three days. In the end, they voted against it. The scope of the convention had changed. The delegates weren't going to revise an old government model. They were going to build a brand new one.

Representation and the Great Compromise

The Virginia Plan called for a legislative (or lawmaking) branch of government made up of two houses. Delegates from the large states wanted representation in the House of Representatives to be based on population. Delegates from small states, seeing the disadvantage this would cause them, wanted each state to have an equal number of representatives in the House.

The taxation issue added fuel to the fiery debates. Together, the questions of taxation and representation highlighted the differences not only between large and small states, but also between Northern and Southern states. Southern states had large slave populations. They did not want to have to pay more taxes

Fact Finder

Before you read (or reread) this section, set a purpose for your reading. Here are some questions to think about:

✓ Why is representation a controversial issue?

✓ What groups need to compromise?

✓ What is the compromise?

✓ Is it beneficial for both sides?

Consider situations where you've had to work out a compromise. Discuss/compare these experiences with your classmates.

The Assembly Room of Independence Hall *(above)* is where the Constitution, the Declaration of Independence, and the Articles of Confederation were drafted, debated, and signed.

because of slaves, whom they considered inferior laborers, not citizens.

Connecticut delegate Oliver Ellsworth helped break the deadlock on July 12, with a proposal that representation in the House of Representatives be calculated based on "free persons" and "three-fifths of all other persons" (meaning slaves). This proposal, which would come to be known as the Great Compromise, or the Connecticut Compromise, met with approval. On its heels, three major agreements were reached:

• Direct taxation would be based on representation.
• Representation in the House of Representatives would be calculated according to a state's white inhabitants and three-fifths of its "other people."
• Each state would have equal number of representatives in the Senate (regardless of population).

Commerce and Slavery

With major issues resolved and major aspects of the government taking shape, a Committee of Detail was created. This committee would prepare a draft of the Constitution, reflecting decisions made by the convention so far. While the Committee of Detail worked on this draft, the other delegates enjoyed a ten-day break from the pressures of the convention.

The delegates came back from their break to review the rough draft submitted by the Committee of Detail on August 6, 1787. Regulation of commerce proved to be a sticking point. Southern states were concerned that regulation of trade by a strong central government—especially if dominated by large, Northern states—would hinder the South's economy, particularly its export business.

On August 21, an economic discussion turned into an ethical discussion when Maryland delegate Luther Martin

Word Works

✓ **abolish** To end or destroy.

✓ **ethical** Involving or expressing moral approval or disapproval.

✓ **hinder** To block, obstruct, or slow the progress of.

People fighting for the abolition, or end, of slavery were called abolitionists. "Abolish" is the root of both words.

African slaves labor in cotton fields on a plantation in the American South.

proposed a tax on the importing of slaves. The institution of slavery was called into question. Once again, the convention seemed to be in jeopardy because of issues that divided Northern and Southern states. Once again, compromise prevented deadlock:

- Northern states agreed to allow the importing of slaves for twenty years (in spite of moral concerns about slavery and the negative effect this agreement would have on the fight to abolish slavery).
- Southern states agreed that navigation laws could be made by majority vote in Congress (in spite of their concerns that this would give Northern states too much control over regulation of trade).

Solutions and Signatures

At the end of August, the convention was winding down. Remember, the delegates had been debating, fighting, and writing for three intense months. A final hurdle had to be cleared. There were many different opinions about how to elect the chief executive, or president. Proposals included the following:

- Direct election by the public
- Election by state legislatures
- Election by state governors
- Election by Congress

Q & A

✓ Would you have put your signature on the Constitution if you had been at the convention on September 17, 1787? Why or why not?

✓ Why do you think Randolph, Mason, and Gerry called for a new convention?

✓ How do you think American history would be different if the delegates had not approved the Constitution?

The winning solution was the electoral college, which is the method we use to elect the president and vice president to this day.

With that issue put to rest, it was time to finalize the document that would become the United States Constitution. Gouverneur Morris was appointed head of the Committee of Style. On September 12, the Committee of Style presented its revised version of the Constitution to the delegates. The delegates went through this version with a fine-tooth comb, reviewing each section. On September 15, it was time for the delegates to vote on the final Constitution. Three delegates (Edmund Randolph, George Mason, and Elbridge Gerry) felt another convention should be held to tackle the work afresh. They were in the minority, though, and the Constitution was approved.

Benjamin Franklin wrote a speech to mark the last day of the convention, September 17, 1787. Since he was in poor health, another delegate delivered the speech, which was intended to rally support for the Constitution. However imperfect, the Constitution was a thoughtfully written, fairly debated proposal for a promising new government. Thirty-nine of the fifty-five delegates signed the document. The delegates' work was done. Now, the American people would have to decide the Constitution's fate.

Benjamin Franklin *(above)* offered the following thoughts on the Constitution in his closing convention speech: "I agree to this Constitution with all its faults, if they are such; because I think a general Government necessary for us . . . I doubt too whether any other Convention we can obtain, may be able to make a better Constitution."

Taking Sides

Picture this! A seven-page document is printed and circulated in America. American citizens have to review the document and decide if they are willing to accept it. If the majority of the citizens ratify, everyone will have to follow the rules in the document. That was the scene in America in September 1787. Americans had many different opinions about the Constitution. They expressed their opinions in several ways. Some people wrote newspaper articles. Political cartoons illustrated other people's points of view. Pamphlets were filled with still other ideas. The stakes were high. The decision was difficult. People were using the media to express points of view. Does this sound like a scene that could take place today? If so, in what way?

If you were an American citizen in 1787, you would have to pick a side. Two main camps formed.

Get Graphic

✓ Under the Articles of Confederation, how many branches of government are there?

  a. two

  b. three

  c. one

  d. five

✓ How are taxes handled under the Constitution?

  a. Congress does not have power to tax.

  b. Congress does have power to tax.

  c. State governments handle taxes.

  d. Local governments handle taxes.

Differences Between the Articles of Confederation and the Constitution

Issue	Articles of Confederation	U.S. Constitution
Central Government	Weak	Strong
Relationship of States	Loose confederation	Union
National Leader	None	President
Branches	One	Three
Congress	One house	Two houses
Money	States and Congress issue money	Only Congress issues money
Taxes	Congress does not have power to tax	Congress has power to tax
Trade	Each state handles own trade	National government handles trade
Courts	No Supreme Court	Court system includes Supreme Court

People who wanted a strong central government were called Federalists. They agreed with the ideas in the new constitution. The anti-Federalists did not want a strong central government. They preferred the decentralized government of the Articles of Confederation. They opposed the new constitution. Take a look at some of the other key issues.

America Decides

There were only thirteen states in America in 1787. Nine of those states had to ratify the Constitution for it to go into effect. Nine may not seem like a big number, but those nine states represented many conflicting, or differing, concerns and issues. It took a year, but America finally decided. The required nine states ratified the Constitution. The road to ratification had not been smooth or easy. In the end, though, Americans decided to make the Constitution the new law of the land.

- What is the story of this political cartoon?
- Can you describe it in words?
- What is the artist comparing the United States to?
- Do you think this is an effective picture? Why or why not?

Get Graphic

✓ **What does the artist think will happen if all thirteen states ratify the Constitution?**

a. The United States will become stronger.

b. Some states will be more powerful than others.

c. The United States will fall apart.

d. The states will be independent but cooperative.

TINEL   VOL. 1

REDEUNT SATURNIA REGNA.

...on of the Eleventh PILLAR of the great Na-

..., we beg leave most sincerely to felicitate " OUR DEAR COUNTRY."

Rise it will.

The foundation good—it may yet be SAVED.

The *FEDERAL EDIFICE*.

ELEVEN STARS, in quick succession rise—
ELEVEN COLUMNS strike our wond'ring eyes,
Soon o'er the *whole*, shall swell the beauteous DOME,
COLUMBIA's boast—and FREEDOM's hallow'd home.
   Here shall the ARTS in glorious splendour shine!
And AGRICULTURE give her stores divine!
COMMERCE refin'd, dispense us more than gold,
And this new world, teach WISDOM to the old—
RELIGION here shall fix her blest abode,
Array'd in *mildness*, like its parent GOD!
JUSTICE and LAW, shall endless PEACE maintain,
And the " SATURNIAN AGE," *return again*.

This political cartoon celebrates the ratification of the Constitution by New York on July 26, 1778. At this point, the only two states who had yet to ratify were North Carolina and Rhode Island. Rhode Island was the last of the original thirteen states to ratify the Constitution (on May 29, 1790), doing so only after being threatened with greater taxation.

The Bill of Rights

Once the Constitution was ratified, there was still room for improvement. The delegates had made a provision to allow amendments, meaning changes or additions, to be made to the Constitution. This provision allowed the first ten amendments to be added to the Constitution. James Madison organized suggestions submitted by the states. In their final form, these ten amendments would become the Bill of Rights as we know it today.

Think Tank

✓ Team up with classmates to study the First and Fourth Amendments and then rewrite them in your own words (using modern language!).

✓ Assign roles like reader, researcher, and writer.

✓ Use classroom resources to help figure out tough words or ideas.

✓ What freedoms does each amendment protect?

✓ Why are these rights important for American citizens?

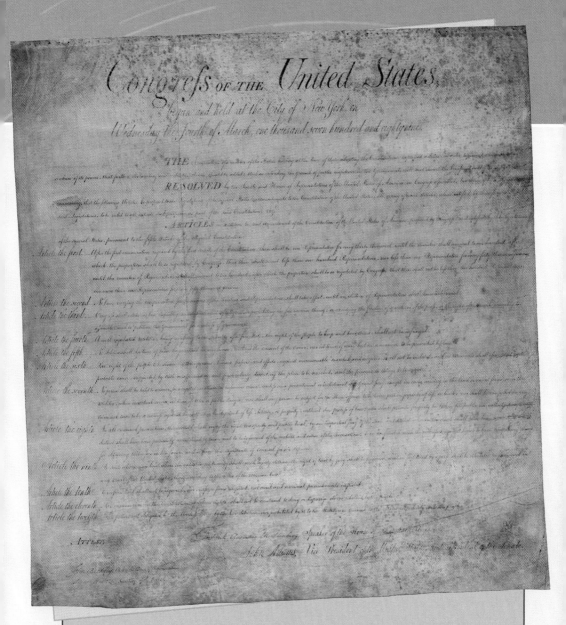

When some states ratified the U.S. Constitution, they also asked for additional amendments to the document to protect the individual freedoms of citizens from possible government tyranny. Ten of these amendments became known as the Bill of Rights. The document introducing these amendments (*above*) begins with the words, "The Conventions of a number of the States, having at the time of their adopting the Constitution, expressed a desire, in order to prevent misconstruction or abuse of its powers, that further declaratory and restrictive clauses should be added."

A Living Document

It was a long summer of debate and disagreement, compromise and controversy, drafts and revisions. But in the end, the Constitutional Convention delegates accomplished their mission. They came up with an innovative, effective plan for America's government. The document they constructed has been the backbone of America's government for more than 200 years. Through the years, changes have been made to the Constitution. But, by and large, the document reads today much as it did then. The men whose signatures are on the Constitution have faded into the pages of history, but their ideas live on in the Constitution.

Paper Works

✓ Take a look at a copy or transcription of the Constitution.

✓ Study an article closely.

✓ Write a two-part essay based on your understanding of that article.

✓ How does it affect you personally (as a citizen)?

✓ How does the article address, or relate to, a current issue or problem? (You can apply the article to a school, local, or national issue.)

The National Archives *(above)* in Washington, D.C., houses many of America's most important historical documents, including the Declaration of Independence, the Articles of Confederation, the Constitution, and the Bill of Rights.

Timeline

| 1775 | 1781 | 1783 | 1786 | May 25, 1787 | May 29, 1787 | June 13, 1787 |

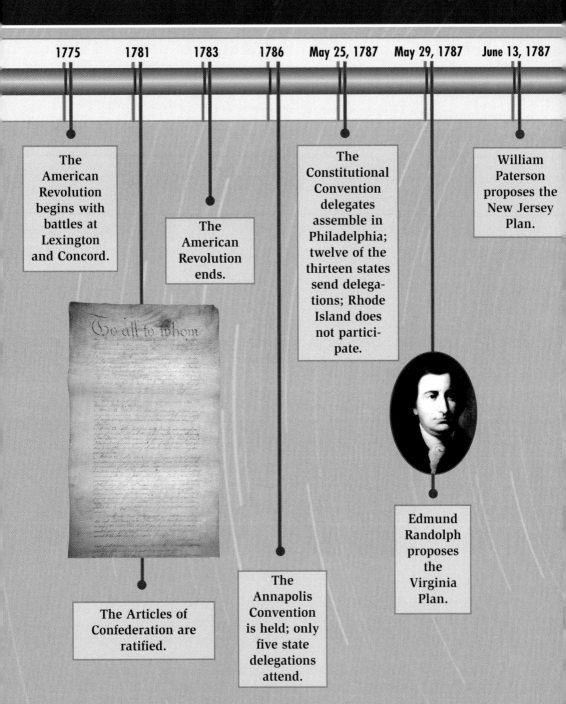

The American Revolution begins with battles at Lexington and Concord.

The American Revolution ends.

The Constitutional Convention delegates assemble in Philadelphia; twelve of the thirteen states send delegations; Rhode Island does not participate.

William Paterson proposes the New Jersey Plan.

Edmund Randolph proposes the Virginia Plan.

The Articles of Confederation are ratified.

The Annapolis Convention is held; only five state delegations attend.

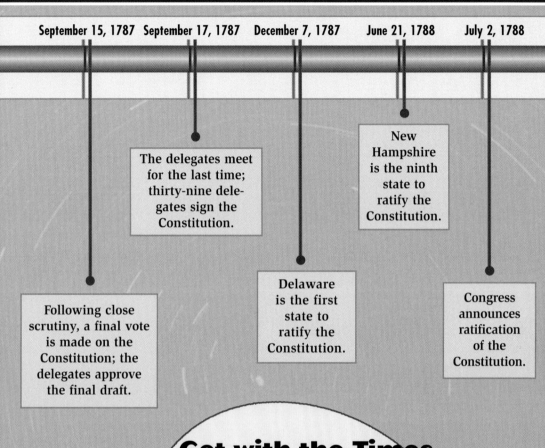

September 15, 1787 · September 17, 1787 · December 7, 1787 · June 21, 1788 · July 2, 1788

The delegates meet for the last time; thirty-nine delegates sign the Constitution.

New Hampshire is the ninth state to ratify the Constitution.

Following close scrutiny, a final vote is made on the Constitution; the delegates approve the final draft.

Delaware is the first state to ratify the Constitution.

Congress announces ratification of the Constitution.

Get with the Times

Check out the timeline to answer these questions.

✓ When did the Constitutional Convention start?

✓ When did the delegates sign the Constitution?

✓ Which state was the first to ratify the Constitution?

Graphic Organizers in Action

Venn Diagram

BIG STATES
- ✓ favor strong central government
- ✓ want a union of states
- ✓ want balance of power to favor national government, not individual states
- ✓ want representation in Congress to be based on population

(overlap)
- ✓ want protection of individual citizens' rights
- ✓ need a stable economy
- ✓ need national security
- ✓ want regulation of trade

SMALL STATES
- ✓ favor weaker central government
- ✓ want a confederation of states
- ✓ want balance of power to favor individual states, not national government
- ✓ want representation in Congress to be equal for all states

SEQUENCE CHART

- ✓ American dissatisfaction with British rule
- ✓ The American Revolutionary War
- ✓ The Articles of Confederation
- ✓ Problems with trade, finance, and national instability under the Articles of Confederation

- ✓ The Annapolis Convention
- ✓ The Madison/Hamilton letter inviting states to national convention
- ✓ Congress makes formal resolution calling for national a convention

- ✓ Delegates assemble at the Philadelphia State House
- ✓ George Washington is elected chairman of the convention
- ✓ Randolph introduces the Virginia Plan
- ✓ Paterson introduces the New Jersey Plan

Controversial issues are debated and resolved:
- ✓ Power and structure of central government
- ✓ Representation
- ✓ How slaves will be counted in terms of representation and taxes
- ✓ Regulation of trade
- ✓ The delegates complete the Constitution
- ✓ The Constitution is submitted to Congress
- ✓ Congress submits it to the states

K W L Chart

What I Know	What I Want to Know	What I've Learned
✓ America has a strong central government today. ✓ The government is made up of three branches. ✓ Our government operates according to a document called the Constitution. ✓ The Constitution was written more than 200 years ago, but it is still in effect today.	✓ Why does America have such a powerful central government? ✓ Why is the government made up of three branches? ✓ Who wrote the Constitution? How and why did they write it? ✓ America's needs and issues are always changing. How can the Constitution, written so long ago, still be effective today?	✓ Much thought and debate went into the decision to make America's central government so powerful. ✓ The three branches are intended to act as checks and balances. The Founding Fathers did not want to end up with an oppressive government, like the British government that had ruled the American colonies. ✓ The Founding Fathers, who wrote the Constitution, were mostly well-educated, wealthy politicians who held leadership roles in America's colonial and state governments. ✓ The framers of the Constitution created it to be a flexible document. They built in provisions for making changes to the document over time.

Get Graphic

✓ Study these examples of graphic organizers.

✓ They organize information about the creation of the Constitution.

✓ Can you build a Venn diagram, KWL chart, and sequence chart to organize information about the ratification of the Constitution?

(For example, you could use the Venn diagram to illustrate the positions of the Federalists and anti-Federalists.)

Glossary

advocate (AD-vuh-kit) Someone who defends or pleads for a certain cause or proposal.

agenda (uh-JEN-duh) A list of things to be considered or done.

colony (KAH-lun-ee) A body of people living in a new territory that is governed by a parent state.

commerce (KAH-mers) The buying and selling of goods.

confederation (kun-fed-uh-RAY-shun) The act of coming together to form a league of nations, or the league of nations itself.

constitution (kahn-stih-TOO-shun) The basic principles and laws of a nation or state, which detail the government's powers and duties and the rights of citizens.

credential (kree-DEN-chul) Something that establishes someone's trustworthiness or suitability.

debate (dih-BAYT) Formal discussion or argument about an issue or a proposition.

debts (DETS) Money that is owed.

decentralized government (DEE-sen-trul-iyzd GUH-vern-mint) An administration that has power spread out over a large number of regional governments, rather than one powerful, central government.

economy (ee-KAH-nuh-mee) The way a country or business manages its resources.

export (EKS-port) To send something outside of one's country.

federal (FEH-duh-rul) Relating to a central or national government rather than individual or state governments.

legislature (LEH-jis-lay-chur) A lawmaking body.

proceedings (pro-SEE-dings) Events or happenings, often of a legal sort.

ratify (RAH-ti-fy) To formally approve, as in a law.

sabotage (SAB-ih-taj) An act of destruction designed to hurt or hamper the established order.

Web Sites

Due to the changing nature of Internet links, the Rosen Publishing Group, Inc., has developed an online list of Web sites related to the subject of this book. This site is updated regularly. Please use this link to access the list:

http://www.rosenlinks.com/ctah/drco

For Further Reading

Aten, Jerry, and Robert Greisen. *Our Living Constitution: Then and Now*. Carthage, IL: Good Apple, Inc., 2001.

Burnett, Betty. *The Continental Congress: A Primary Source History of the Formation of America's New Government*. New York, NY: The Rosen Publishing Group, Inc., 2004.

Callahan, Kerry P. *The Articles of Confederation: A Primary Source Investigation into the Document that Preceded the U.S. Constitution*. New York, NY: The Rosen Publishing Group, Inc., 2003.

Freedman, Russell. *In Defense of Liberty: The Story of America's Bill of Rights*. New York, NY: Holiday House, 2003.

Giddens, Sandra, and Owen Giddens. *A Timeline of the Constitutional Convention*. New York, NY: The Rosen Publishing Group, Inc., 2003.

Hossell, Karen Price. *The United States Constitution*. Chicago, IL: Heinemann Library, 2003.

Hughes, Christopher. *The Constitutional Convention*. San Diego, CA: Blackbirch Press, 2004.

Quiri, Patricia Ryon. *The Constitution*. New York, NY: Children's Press, 1999.

Weidner, Daniel. *Creating the Constitution: The People and Events That Formed the Nation*. Berkeley Heights, NJ: Enslow Publishers, 2002.

Index

About the Author

Kristin Eck is the author of more than a dozen books for the Rosen Publishing Group. She is a particularly keen student of America's colonial era, an interest that finds especially rewarding outlet in Pennsylvania's history-rich Bucks County, where she lives with her husband and two children.

Photo Credits: Cover left, p. 27 © Lester Lefkowitz/Corbis; cover right © Catherine Karnow/Corbis; pp. 5, 7, 15, 19, 31 © Bettmann/Corbis; pp. 9, 23, 37, 40 © National Archives and Records Administration, Washington, DC; p. 11 © Worcester Art Museum, MA, USA/Bridgeman Art Library; p. 13 © MPI/Getty Images; pp. 17, 21, 25, 35 © Library of Congress; p. 29 © Corbis; p. 39 © Lee Snider/Photo Images/Corbis.

Designer: Nelson Sá; Photo Researcher: Nelson Sá